20,000 Leagues Under the Sea

Adapted by: FRANCINE HUGHES
Illustrated by: ANNI MATSICK

© Binney & Smith. Crayola Kids Adventures is a trademark of Binney & Smith. All rights reserved.
Printed in the U.S.A. No part of this book may be reproduced or copied in any form
without written permission from the copyright owner.

GOLDEN BOOKS®, A GOLDEN BOOK®, G DESIGN™, and the distinctive gold spine
are trademarks of Golden Books Publishing Company, Inc. New York, NY 10106
Library Of Congress Catalog Number: 97-74207
ISBN: 0-307-20200-3   A MCMXCVII

Message for Readers:

Reading is fun! It allows you to go on adventures, learn about fascinating places, and meet new people without ever leaving your chair. And the fun doesn't have to stop after you have finished reading the book. With Crayola® Kids Adventures™ chapter books you can let your imagination run wild. Consider these other ways to add your ideas to the story so the adventure can last as long as you like.

• Design a new cover for this book. Create an exciting scene that would attract other readers to this story.

• Challenge yourself to come up with two or three different endings for this book. What might have turned the events around? How can you include new characters in the story to change the direction of the plot?

• This story was written a long time ago. Imagine you are the writer and it was written this year. How would you weave modern technology, current events, and popular products into your tale.

• Start a Readers Club. Invite your friends and tell them to read the story ahead of time. Ask them to dress as their favorite character, and to bring their creative endings and book covers to the party. Then have everyone share their thoughts on the story.

Crayola Kids Adventures Products

The Crayola Kids Adventures series starts with quality literature and weaves in activities to make learning fun. Because everyone learns differently, Crayola Kids Adventures has multiple approaches and types of activities to help you learn. Look for these other Crayola Kids Adventures products:

- IBM Computer Software

- Crayola Kids Adventures Videos

- Crayola, Arts & Activity Kits

- Revell Monogram Nautilus Modeling Kit

- Crayola Kids Adventures Magazine

- Plymouth Specialty and Drawing Papers

- Other Hallmark Home Entertainment Videos

CHAPTER 1

In 1866 people were scared.

They were scared because something strange and mysterious was said to be living under the ocean. Something big. And mean. With glowing green eyes. People said it was a monster! It was huge, with a long spear sticking out of its nose. This monster would chase ships all over the seas, and then it would poke its spear straight into them. No one had ever actually seen the monster. But everyone knew it was out there. All of the sailors on the high seas were afraid to cross the ocean in fear of this horrible monster.

Admiral Selling of the United States Navy decided something must be done about this monster before it scared away any more ships. But what? She needed help, so she went to the American Museum of Natural History in New York City. She wanted to see a young professor there named Dr. Pierre Arronax.

When Admiral Selling arrived, Dr. Arronax was in his office peering at an old bone. He looked very serious. His sister, Beth, peeked over his shoulder. Admiral Selling knocked at the door and poked her head inside.

"I've heard about you," she said to Professor Arronax and his sister. "You are the only people in the whole world who might know how to find the monster that is living in the sea!"

The professor put down his bone. "Frankly, admiral, I've never found a monster."

"You haven't?" the admiral asked, somewhat surprised.

The professor shook his head. "No, because there aren't any. They do not exist."

"B-b-but," the admiral stuttered, "people have told me about this one!"

"Baloney!" the professor said. "You cannot trust the human eye."

"You see," Beth interrupted, "my brother only believes in cold hard facts."

"Right," the professor agreed. "Facts."

"My brother believes science holds the answer to everything, " Beth continued.

"Right." The professor nodded. "Science is the key."

"And my brother has a big fat head," joked Beth.

"Righto," said the professor. "My head is unusually large . . . "

He stopped short. "Hey! Wait a minute!"

The admiral held up her hand. "I'm not sure about your head, Professor. But I do know there is something loose on the high seas. And everyone says it is a monster."

The professor and Beth looked at each other. Then the professor nodded to Beth. She took out a pad and pencil. She was ready to take notes. "How big?" she asked.

"Over three hundred feet," the admiral replied.

"Three hundred feet!" Beth exclaimed. "That's bigger than the biggest whale, larger than the largest dinosaur."

"Impossible!" the professor exclaimed. "Unless it's—"

"A monster!" cried the admiral.

"No," Beth said calmly. "Unless it's a new animal. One that hasn't been discovered yet."

"Exactly!" the professor grinned. He paced back and forth. "I could discover this animal. This unknown species. It could be the high point of my career."

"Then you'll join us!" the admiral exclaimed. "The USS *Abraham Lincoln* sets sail at sunset, with orders to find this monster."

"You mean, unknown species," the professor corrected.

"Call it what you want, Professor," said the admiral. "The U.S. Navy needs your help."

The professor stepped forward. "Count me in!"

Beth joined him. "Count *us* in!"

CHAPTER 2

Night fell over the ocean. The ship plowed through the dark, choppy sea. The professor stood at the railing. Mist sprayed his face. Beside him, Beth gazed out over the waves.

"This is the fastest, newest ship in the Navy," Captain Farragut, the commander of the ship, explained. As usual, he was sharply dressed in a crisp uniform.

"We have to find the creature," he said, looking out at the sea. The captain was worried. He wanted to capture the creature, but he was not so sure he wanted to run into it.

Beth reached into a big suitcase. She pulled out a device with wires and spinning dials. It was called the *double-helix dual-flex audio confibulator.*

"The creature may be a whale," she told the captain. "If it is, it would make sounds. This machine can hear them. So we just follow the sounds. And then we'll find it."

"Splendid!" said the captain, watching her set up the machine.

"It will never work," a voice behind them called.

The professor and Beth spun around.

Ned Land stepped into view. He was the ship's harpoonist. Ned was a bit of an outsider. He didn't talk to many of the sailors on the ship. He just kept to himself. He wanted to do his job and be left alone.

"I said, it will never work," Ned repeated.

The professor eyed Ned. He took in his ragged pants and shirt. Who was this sailor? What did he know?

"I suppose you're an expert?" the professor asked.

Ned met his gaze. "Well, I know the ocean. And you won't find a monster with that," he said pointing to the device.

20,000 LEAGUES UNDER THE SEA

The captain cleared his throat. "Professor, Beth, I'd like you to meet Ned Land."

"Best harpoonist on the seven seas," Ned said. He lifted his harpoon. "Get me close to the critter," he told the captain, "and we'll have that monster on a stick in no time."

Beth narrowed her eyes. "And how do *you* think we can find it?"

Ned grinned. "By smell. All monsters stink."

"Baloney!" cried the professor. "You cannot trust the human nose."

"Besides," Beth added, "how do you know monsters stink?"

"Have you ever seen one take a bath?" asked Ned.

"Why, no," Beth said.

Ned crossed his arms, satisfied. "I rest my case," he said.

"Then you have seen a monster?" the professor said to Ned.

"I've heard stories," Ned said. He spoke in a strong,

confident voice. "Stories about creatures who eat ships in one bite. And sea serpents. And flying octopuses."

The professor laughed. "Gibberish!"

Just then the captain gasped.

"M-m-m-monster!" he yelled.

CHAPTER 3

All of the crew rushed on deck. They raced to the railing and stared out at where the captain was pointing. Beth and the professor scanned the water.

Suddenly, two green, glowing eyes rose up from the waves.

The professor squinted. It was very dark over the ocean. He could barely see a thing. But those eyes! They held his gaze—and they were coming closer. Everyone was quiet.

The monster cut through the water like a knife, moving swiftly toward the ship.

"Battle stations!" the captain shouted, breaking the silence. "Prepare for action!"

The crew sprang to life. They scurried around looping ropes and tightening hatches.

E-o-e-o-e-o! The ship's siren blared its warning sound.

"Cannons!" ordered the captain.

Sailors hauled the giant guns out on deck and aimed them at the glowing eyes, which were getting closer and closer.

Ned gripped his harpoon. He strode to the bow of the ship, ready to take aim at the beast.

The creature churned closer.

The professor grabbed a pen and scribbled notes. Beth pulled out a measuring device and pointed it at the creature.

"It measures three-hundred-twenty-seven feet!" she cried out in surprise. "What is it?"

"I-I-I don't know!" the professor stammered.

The creature sped closer and closer.

"Ready the cannons!" the captain called out. "Fire on my command!"

The sea parted. Water spouted up in a fountain and the monster shot forward at an even faster pace.

Beth grabbed the notepad. She did some quick figuring. "Yikes! That creature's going over sixty miles per hour!"

"Impossible!" the professor shouted. "Nothing moves that fast."

It seemed impossible, but the creature *was* moving at an incredibly fast pace. It had almost reached the ship!

The captain turned to his gunners. "Aim!" he cried. Now they could see the creature's long round shape and make out the pointed spear on its head.

Ned held his harpoon tightly. "Come on, you slimy bottom-dweller!" he whispered as he waited for his chance to take on the creature.

"Fire!" the captain shouted.

A loud roar echoed through the ship. Cannonballs exploded. One, two, three direct hits.

But every hit bounced off the creature! Nothing could

20,000 LEAGUES UNDER THE SEA

stop it. The creature continued to get closer to the ship.

The captain grew pale. Cannonballs did nothing. What kind of beast was this? He stepped back, afraid. What could they do?

Ned leaped onto the railing. This was his chance. Now, before the monster struck.

"Hey, you overgrown guppy!" he called as he tossed the harpoon. It soared through the air. Everyone's eyes followed the harpoon, hoping that it would finally stop the creature.

Pffft! It whacked the creature. And just like the cannonballs, it bounced right off.

The monster lunged towards the ship. Any second it would attack.

Any second—

Just then there was a loud crash. The monster rammed the ship. Its spear pierced the wood and iron. The boat shuddered and rocked back and forth.

"Ahhh!" Ned screamed as he tottered off the railing and plunged into the sea.

The monster pulled back a bit, but it was too late. Water gushed through the hole that the monster had made. Waves swept onto the deck. There was terrible confusion. The crew tried to bail out the water. The captain tried to restore order.

"Man the pumps!" cried the captain. "Seal the doors!"

A wall of water—a tidal wave—smashed over the railing. Everything in its path *whooshed* out to sea, including everyone on deck.

Beth and the professor tried to hold on. But the force was too strong, and they, too, tumbled into the deep, dark ocean, toward the terrible monster.

CHAPTER 4

The professor floated back to the surface. He flailed around, searching for the ship. He saw it, off in the distance, leaning to one side. It had taken in a lot of water, but it was still sailing.

Sailing away!

"Beth! Ned!" he shouted, paddling toward the ship. Where were the others? Were they sailing away without him?

"Professor!" Ned called.

"Over here!" cried Beth.

The professor swam toward the voices. He found Beth and Ned floating nearby, holding on to a wooden plank.

Beth smiled at her brother. "Thank goodness you're all right," she cried.

"Thank goodness I learned to swim," the professor said, grabbing onto the plank.

The ship's horn blasted. The three turned and watched the ship sail away.

"Now what?" Beth cried, alarmed at the fact that the creature could be close by.

"Hold on tight," Ned said. "Somebody will find us sooner or later."

Suddenly they heard a rumbling. It was a noise like a ship's engine.

"Looks like somebody found us," Beth said, relieved.

Just then the creature rose from the depths of the water.

"It's the monster!" shouted the professor.

The giant, gray-green creature loomed near. Water sprayed everywhere, drenching the professor, Beth, and Ned. They held on to the plank tightly.

Then, right in front of them, the creature stopped.

It floated, still as a statue.

"Don't move," Beth whispered.

"Maybe it's not hungry," Ned said hopefully.

"Maybe it's not a monster," the professor said thoughtfully. He peered over at it. "Look! It's made of iron!" he cried.

Curious, the three floated towards the mysterious object. They stared at it for a long time. Beth shivered. The water was freezing. And she'd had enough of it.

"Follow me," she commanded.

Beth swam forward. The professor and Ned exchanged nervous looks, then followed her orders and paddled behind her. A moment later, they climbed onto the thing. It was smooth and cool to the touch.

"It *is* made of iron!" Ned exclaimed. "But what is it?"

Just then a door swung open.

A greenish glow streamed out.

Beth shrugged. She looked at her brother. "We've come this far . . ."

Her voice trailed off as she pointed to the opening.

"Are you crazy?" Ned hissed. "We don't know what's in there!"

"Exactly!" The professor said, and grinned, excited. This was just what he liked, exploring something new and discovering something different.

"All right," Ned sighed. "But what if we get eaten? I'm never talking to either of you again."

One by one, the three climbed inside the hatch and down the ladder. Then they edged their way through another door. They seemed to be going deeper and deeper inside of the thing.

Then, suddenly, all three stopped dead in their tracks.

CHAPTER 5

They had entered some kind of control room. Ned gazed around the chamber. Dials and switches and levers lined the walls. Strange gadgets—all with flashing buttons and pointing arrows—were everywhere. There was a large steering wheel, and a big captain's chair stood behind it.

"It seems impossible," the professor exclaimed, "but this must be a suboceanic craft. A submarine!"

The chair swung around. "Very good," said the captain, startling them.

Two crewmen quietly entered the room. They stood on either side of the captain.

"Who are you?" Beth asked bravely, as she huddled next to the professor and Ned.

The captain stood and bowed. "My name is Nemo. I'm the captain of the *Nautilus*, the world's first submarine."

"It *is* a submarine!" the professor and Beth said together. "Wow!"

The professor could not believe his good luck. He wanted to know all about the submarine. "How deep can you go? What type of engine do you have? How do you breathe?" he asked, all at once.

Nemo held up his hand. "Please. I'm not here to answer your questions. I am only here to right a wrong."

Ned stepped forward. "And what wrong is that, flounder face? You came to kill us!"

"I never wanted to harm anyone," Nemo answered. "I just wanted to warn Captain Farragut. Tell him to leave me alone."

The professor eyed the silent crewmen, trying to take

in the situation. He then met the captain's firm gaze. There was no doubt about it, these people meant business. "Are we prisoners?" he asked, not wanting to believe it.

Nemo shook his head. "No. I will give you a lifeboat, some food and water. A ship will rescue you, I am sure."

Leave the world's first submarine without having the chance to explore it? The professor didn't want that. He wanted to investigate. "Couldn't we ride with you for a couple of days?" he asked Nemo.

Ned shot the professor a look. "In this bucket of bolts? Underwater?" He laughed. "What are you, crazy?"

"I apologize for my friend," the professor said quickly. "I'm Professor Arronax," he said, introducing himself and the others to Captain Nemo. Then he looked around the chamber. "I'd love to come with you."

Nemo nodded. "You are all welcome to stay. If you come with me you will learn secrets beyond your wildest dreams." He paused. "But these secrets come with a price."

"A price?" Beth repeated nervously, not quite sure that she liked the sound of that.

Just then a great explosion ripped through the sub. Nemo gave a signal to his crew, and they raced to the control board. One pulled a lever. Another twisted a knob.

A long tube bent at the bottom, came down.

"A periscope!" said the professor.

Nemo peered through the opening. Through it he could see the ocean's surface, even though he was under the water. Then he saw the USS *Abraham Lincoln* chugging closer. It had returned to look for the professor, Beth, and Ned.

Then there was another explosion! The USS *Abraham Lincoln* was attacking the submarine!

The submarine shook.

"It seems that Captain Farragut," Nemo said quietly, "has not understood my warning."

"What are you going to do?" the professor asked.

Nemo shrugged. "Nothing. I have more important things to do."

He pressed a button. Then he turned to the three visitors.

"The choice is yours," Nemo said. "You can still have my lifeboat. Maybe your friends on the ship will be able to save you. Or you can come with me."

All of a sudden there was a great bang. The cannons roared again. There was no way a little lifeboat would be safe out there.

"We'll stick with you," said Ned.

CHAPTER 6

With that, the *Nautilus* began to plunge below the surface, going deeper and deeper toward the ocean floor.

Nemo turned to his guests. "We're at three hundred feet," he said.

"Underwater?" Ned gasped.

Nemo smiled. "The *Nautilus* can go deeper."

"This is plenty deep for me," Ned replied.

"Dinner will be served in two hours," Nemo said. "Until then, you are free to explore. My home is your home."

Ned reached for a flashing button on the control board.

"Just don't touch anything!" Nemo ordered sternly.

The professor, Beth, and Ned were shown to their quarters a few minutes later. They changed out of their

wet clothes and into the dry *Nautilus* uniforms that the crew gave them.

Now, the professor thought, *it's time to explore.* He could not wait.

The three visitors wandered up and down hallways. There were so many blinking lights, so many strange devices. Ned eyed a machine with three long glass tubes. Bright red water bubbled inside each one. He reached out to touch them, but Beth grabbed his wrist.

"I was just trying to figure it out," Ned explained.

"It's an oxygen-recycling system," Beth told him.

Ned scratched his head. "An oxo-what?"

"Oxygen recycling," Beth repeated. "It takes air out of the water so we can breathe."

"Like a fish uses gills?" Ned asked.

"Exactly."

Ned whistled. "Amazing!"

The professor stuck his head through another doorway. "You think that's amazing? Look in here!"

Beth and Ned scurried to join him. They entered a larger chamber. Dozens of paintings hung on the walls. Statues and vases and pieces of art were everywhere.

"It's like a museum!" Beth spoke in a whisper.

The three walked along looking at a wall covered with art. Some paintings looked familiar. The professor felt sure he'd seen them in art books. *They must be paintings done by famous artists*, he thought. *And statues carved by famous sculptors.*

Beth stopped in front of a statue against a wall. It was of a man's head.

"This has been lost for over one hundred years!" she exclaimed.

The professor strode over. "It sank with a ship!"

Ned rubbed the statue's head. "I bet it's worth a pretty penny now," he said.

"Ned!" Beth warned. "Don't touch anything. Remember Nemo's warning!"

Ned laughed. "Nemo, Schlemo. What's it going to hurt?"

He squeezed the statue's nose. Instantly, the wall spun around. It pushed all three around as if they were going through a revolving door.

CHAPTER 7

The professor, Beth, and Ned suddenly found themselves inside a huge empty room.

The chamber was pure white. It was almost blinding. A low buzzing noise bounced off the walls.

In the center, a giant ball hung from the ceiling. A red glow pulsed inside. It seemed to throb in time with the buzzing noise.

Beth edged closer to the ball. "What is it, Professor?"

"I'm not sure," the professor said slowly. He stepped next to Beth. "Let's take a closer look."

Ned sprang over.

"Ned—" Beth began.

"I know! I know!" Ned interrupted. "Don't touch."

He sauntered around the globe. "It looks like a giant upside-down lollipop."

The professor held his hand close to the ball. "It feels warm like the sun."

Beth tilted her head. She listened to the pulse. *Pound, pound, pound.* "It sounds like a heart," she said.

"That's it!" The professor snapped his fingers. "The heart of the ship. This must be the engine. Not a steam engine, like the *Abraham Lincoln*, but one that uses the sun!"

"Still looks like a lollipop to me," Ned muttered.

The buzzing grew louder. The ball glowed brighter. Something was happening.

The three ran back toward the secret wall.

"I got us in here. I can get us out," Ned said.

The door spun around. The professor, Beth, and Ned tumbled with it. It went so fast that they tumbled to the ground. And when they stood up, they could not believe their eyes!

CHAPTER 8

All three had landed in a completely different room! They peered around, gazing at this strange new place. Paintings lined the walls here, too, and sculptures stood on grand pedestals. But this wasn't like the art gallery. This was a much grander room, probably used for very special occasions.

Deep, thick rugs lay on the floor. A chandelier swayed from the ceiling. An organ sat in a corner. There were also bookshelves filled with thousands of books.

"Wow!" Beth sucked in her breath.

"It's like a floating palace," Ned said.

"We're not really floating," Beth told him.

Ned sighed. "Don't remind me," he said, still

uncomfortable with the fact that they were so far under the ocean.

Beth sidled over to the organ. She couldn't help it. She had to touch it. Softly, she stroked a key.

"Bet you can't play," Ned challenged.

"Oh yeah?" Beth struck a loud chord.

Just then a wall panel slid open.

The professor gasped when he saw the window behind it.

"Nemo has a viewing port here!" the professor said. "A place to see the ocean floor!"

The three edged closer to the window. The ocean spread out before them. All sorts of fish, big and small, whirled by. Beams of sunlight lit pretty pink reefs. Plants and vines waved and rippled. Playful dolphins somersaulted into view, and giant sea turtles paddled right up to the window. It was their own private view of the ocean floor, a beautiful, enchanted, underwater world.

20,000 LEAGUES UNDER THE SEA

"Unbelievable," the professor finally said.

"It's like we're in another world," Beth said softly.

"We are," the professor said. "Nemo's world."

"Magnificent, isn't it?" a voice said, startling them all.

The three spun around. Nemo stood behind them.

"I didn't touch anything!" Ned said quickly. "At least not this time."

Nemo chuckled and joined them by the window. A giant octopus floated by and stared straight at them. Then it shot away. A cloud of black ink trailed behind.

"Is this why you built the *Nautilus?*" Beth asked. "To see these sights?"

Nemo shook his head no. "I built it to be free. *Mobilis in mobile.*"

Ned blinked. "Huh?"

"*Mobilis in mobile,*" the professor repeated. "It's Latin. It means free in a free world."

Nemo nodded. "Right you are. And free I am."

Just then the dinner bell rang.

"Come," Nemo said. "We can talk over dinner. I hope you are hungry."

Ned grinned. At last, something that made him happy. "Boy," he said. "I thought you'd never ask."

CHAPTER 9

Huge platters of food covered the dining table. The professor sat next to Nemo. He had so many questions to ask him. He hoped that with all this food they would be there a while, which would give him plenty of time to ask about everything.

The food smelled delicious. Ned scooped up forkful after forkful. The professor dug in too. Finally he finished and was ready to start collecting data.

"The engine," he began. "Is it an aquatic reactor?"

"Yes," Nemo said. "I take fuel from seawater."

"And the paintings and statues?" Beth asked.

"I found them in sunken ships."

Beth put down her fork, looking upset. "So you sink

the ships? Then steal their treasures?"

"No," Nemo answered, getting a little angry. "I'm a collector, not a pirate. I didn't try to sink your ship. I only wanted to scare it away."

Ned munched on a slice of pizza. "I've got a question," he announced.

Nemo turned to him.

"Where'd you get this great pizza? The pepperoni is out of this world!"

Nemo smiled. "That's not pepperoni. It's the left eye of an octopus."

Everyone stopped eating.

Beth pushed away her plate.

"And the spaghetti and meatballs?" Nemo continued. "They're really fish-liver lumps in snake mucus."

He pointed to a tall frothy glass. "And that's a puffer booger milkshake."

He held up the butter tray. "And this is sea horse bellybutton lint.

Everything you see here has been harvested from the sea," Nemo explained. He went on and on, naming the dishes: snail snort stew, earwax of sea snake, and grilled eyeball of starfish.

They tried to be polite and eat. But it wasn't easy. At last Nemo waved for the table to be cleared. The meal was finally over, and they were very relieved.

Now, Nemo announced, it was time to go diving.

CHAPTER 10

Nemo wanted to go diving to gather more food for the next day. Diving on a submarine? Why didn't Nemo just go fishing?

And why did they have to go with him?

Ned put on his diving suit. It fit tightly, like a rubber glove, and the helmet looked like a big round goldfish bowl.

Ned leaned out of the hatch. He gazed at the ocean floor.

"We're really going to walk on the bottom?" he asked doubtfully.

Nemo nodded as he tugged on his helmet.

"How do we breathe?" Beth asked.

"Each suit has a supply of air," Nemo explained.

The professor's eyes glowed. He couldn't wait to get out there.

"We'll be collecting sea urchins," Nemo explained. "Bottom slugs. We only take what we need." He turned to Ned. "And remember — "

"I know!" Ned said. "Don't touch anything!"

"Oh, you can touch," Nemo smiled. "But then you have to eat it."

"I won't touch a thing," Ned promised.

A crewman fastened a lantern to each suit so they could see their way along the dark ocean floor. Then Nemo grabbed a stun gun.

They were off.

Ned floated out the hatch first. He stepped onto the sandy floor, feeling nervous. Deep, green water surrounded him. It seemed so peaceful and quiet. Nothing to be afraid of here.

A group of boulders stood in front of a forest of ferns.

20,000 LEAGUES UNDER THE SEA

Ned and the others headed around the rocks and into the greenery.

Carefully, Nemo picked sea cucumbers from the ground. Then he placed them in a bag he had brought along.

Beth took everything in and sighed happily. She'd never seen such a beautiful place.

She smiled over at Ned. Ned smiled back. But over his shoulder, Beth spied something. Whatever it was, it was coming closer.

Suddenly she gasped. Sharks! Two sharks were headed straight toward Ned!

She frantically waved at Ned to get away. Ned waved back.

Beth shook her head wildly and pointed. Finally Ned turned around. He spotted the sharks. But before he could move, they circled him.

Looking grim, Nemo raised his stun gun. He aimed and fired. Bright blue thunderbolts shot out.

The sharks darted this way and that. They dodged each powerful ray. Then they rushed for Ned again, circling him. Beth paddled around and stood next to the professor, out of the range of fire.

Nemo fired once more. One shark stopped, dazed. But the other crashed right into Ned. Ned toppled over, not able to withstand the full force of the shark.

Nemo let loose another bolt. It cut through the water, hitting the remaining shark head-on. The shark scuttled back. Slowly, it swam away.

Ned staggered to his feet. He gave a thumbs-up sign. He was all right!

Everyone grinned. After that close call, Nemo decided they had done enough diving for the day. Even the professor was happy to go back to the submarine. Moving quickly, they made their way back to the *Nautilus*, and once inside, Beth sighed with relief.

Ned pulled off his helmet. He took a deep breath. "Those sharks almost had me for lunch."

"They need to eat, too," the professor joked.

"Well, they can have my snail snorts," Beth said, laughing.

Everyone took off their diving suits. Then Nemo motioned for them to follow him.

"Come," he said. "I'll show you something better than hungry sharks."

Ned took a deep breath. Anything was better than hungry sharks!

CHAPTER 11

The *Nautilus* cruised along the ocean floor. Nemo checked a dial to make sure that they were on course. He nodded, satisfied. Then he led the others to the viewing port.

The professor peered through the window. A red glow lit the water. There was some kind of light in the distance. In just a few seconds, the color grew brighter. Beth touched the glass.

"It's warm," she said, surprised.

Nemo sat at the organ. He played a little tune while he spoke. "The water is over two hundred and ten degrees," he began.

"My!" said the professor. "That's almost boiling!

20,000 LEAGUES UNDER THE SEA

Where are we, Captain Nemo?"

"We're in a special place. A place people don't believe in," Nemo said mysteriously.

Ruins of an ancient city came into view through the viewing port. Crumbling buildings with white rounded roofs sat next to broken towers with steps that led nowhere.

Behind the city, a great volcano spewed. Red-hot lava flowed into empty streets.

The professor drew in his breath. "The Lost City of Atlantis!" he exclaimed.

"I've heard stories," Ned said. His voice was low, filled with wonder. "It disappeared thousands of years ago."

Nemo struck a chord on the organ. "Mount Atlantis exploded. The city was thrown into the ocean. And still the volcano erupts."

"What a discovery!" cried the professor. He grabbed a notepad and started jotting things down. What a discovery indeed—finding a long-lost city!

"Yeah," Ned added. "I have to tell the boys about this one!"

Nemo frowned. "You won't be telling anyone."

"What?" Ned stared at him.

"I told you before," Nemo replied. "Secrets come with a price."

Beth stepped away from the window. "And what is this price?" she asked.

"You cannot leave," Nemo told her. "If I let you go, you might tell others."

Everyone was silent as this news sunk in. Then Beth spoke up.

"We're prisoners?" she asked.

"Permanent guests," Nemo offered.

The professor gasped. They couldn't leave? Ever?

"You can't keep us here!" he cried, thinking of his research and his lab.

"I can and I will," Nemo said, crossing his arms.

"Why, I ought to . . . " Ned lunged for him.

20,000 LEAGUES UNDER THE SEA

Quickly, Beth and the professor pulled him back, even though they wouldn't have minded taking a shot at Nemo themselves.

As Ned struggled to free himself, Nemo held up his arms, ready to take him on.

CHAPTER 12

Then, suddenly, the submarine jolted.

Everyone stumbled. A loud, horrible screeching
sound echoed through the *Nautilus*.

Beth grabbed the professor. "What is it?" she cried.

Lights flickered. The submarine shook. The noise
was terrible.

Nemo staggered to the window. He looked out at a
frightening sight.

Some kind of sea creature held the sub in its jaws! The
creature was enormous—much, much bigger than any
animal any of them had ever seen. Much bigger than
even the *Nautilus*! Its great mouth gaped open. Its teeth
dug into the submarine. It was sucking them in!

All at once, a blanket of darkness dropped over the window. Nemo pushed a button. Searchlights snapped on. Everyone stepped back in horror.

They were in the creature's mouth! From the window they saw a huge, fleshy mouth, with a giant lolling tongue. Sharp, pointed teeth gnashed together, chomping and chewing on the submarine.

"It looks like the mouth of an Annamayo Tecillian!" the professor shouted.

Beth gripped his hand. "But that creature's been extinct for a hundred million years," she said.

Ned gave a short laugh. "Guess somebody forget to tell *him*!"

The creature shook its head, and the submarine rattled back and forth. Ned slid across the floor.

"I've seen enough!" Ned shouted. He dashed out of the room.

"Come back!" Nemo cried. "We're all in this together!" He turned to chase Ned.

20,000 LEAGUES UNDER THE SEA

A noise like thunder stopped him in his tracks. The monster was grinding the sub in its teeth.

"It's trying to eat us!" the professor yelled.

Nemo reached for a switch. "Then we'll give it indigestion," he said.

White lightning shot out of the sub. Bolt after bolt struck the creature. Electricity crackled through its mouth, over its tongue, and around its teeth. The creature thrashed around in pain.

But it still held on tightly to the submarine.

Everyone tried to brace themselves as the ship continued to shake back and forth.

Nemo trembled with anger and fear. "Nothing! I've shocked it with one hundred million volts and— nothing!" he cried.

There was only one more thing to try.

"Stun guns!" he called to his crew. This was their last hope.

CHAPTER 13

There was only one problem: The stun guns could not be used in the ship. They needed to be directly pointed at the creature. So, minutes later, the crewmen stepped outside, onto the wet lolling tongue of the creature.

Slime poured over the sailors. They slipped, trying to hold their footing. But somehow, they managed to raise their guns and fire.

Powerful rays flew through the monster's pointy teeth and into its gums. The rays were strong enough to stun a hundred sharks.

But not the creature.

"It's not working," Beth moaned, looking on through the viewing port.

20,000 LEAGUES UNDER THE SEA

"Call your men back," the professor warned. "Before it's too late." The professor had figured out the chances of survival, and it did not look good for the sailors if they did not get back inside the submarine as soon as possible.

Just then a flood of water gushed around the sailors. They tumbled and fell. Beth and the professor held their breath. Then, slowly, the sailors managed to get on their feet again. They held on to one another tightly.

Quickly, before another wave struck, Nemo waved them into the sub. He slumped against the controls. "We're beaten," he said.

The professor stared into the creature's mouth. He was trying to figure something out. "Not quite," he said.

"Oh? You have an idea?" Nemo scoffed.

"It's not an idea," the professor answered. "Let's call it a . . . secret."

Beth looked at the creature's mouth and smiled. She knew exactly what the professor was after.

"That's right," she said. "And all secrets have a price."

The creature twisted again, causing the *Nautilus* to rock back and forth.

"And what is the price?" Nemo asked quickly.

"*Mobilis in mobile*," the professor said.

Beth nodded. "Free in a free world," she said.

The professor looked Nemo in the eye. "We promise not to tell anything. Not a word about the *Nautilus* or your discoveries. But we want our freedom."

Nemo was desperate. "Rid me of this monster and I will free you both," he said.

"And Ned?" asked Beth.

Nemo turned red. "He is a fool. I cannot trust him. He will stay."

"No, Ned," the Professor said, "no deal."

The creature tossed its head up and down, still clutching the submarine in its mouth. The submarine shuddered, and Nemo staggered. "All right! You can have Ned. Just tell me the secret."

"This creature does not have a brain," the professor

said. "Only a very simple system that tells it what to do."

The professor paused, trying to decide the best route of action. "Give me five sticks of dynamite," he said with authority.

"What?" said Nemo.

"The explosion will shake up the system—" the professor began.

"—and make it open its jaws," Beth finished. With the creature's jaws open, the ship would be released.

"But we need to place the dynamite carefully," the professor added.

Beth nodded. "Near the roof of the mouth."

Nemo looked unsure. "And how do we get the dynamite there?" he asked, not certain that this would really work.

For a moment there was silence. Then a voice rang out. "You called?"

Ned stood at the door. He had a smile on his face, and a harpoon in his hand.

CHAPTER 14

Ned suited up quickly, since there wasn't a moment to lose. Taking a deep breath, he climbed out the hatch.

The professor and Beth rushed to the viewing port. Nemo stood beside them.

"There he is!" The professor pointed as they watched Ned. Ned steadied himself as he made his way through the creature's mouth.

Ned balanced carefully on the creature's tongue. A bundle of dynamite hung off the end of his harpoon. Slowly he began to climb up the tongue, closer to the roof.

"I was wrong about him," Nemo muttered. "He is very brave. But I hope he can aim!"

A stream of water tossed Ned into the air.

"He'll be swallowed!" Beth cried.

But Ned pulled himself back up. He struggled to his hands and knees. Then, very carefully, he began to crawl. Higher up the tongue. Deeper into the mouth.

Finally he straightened up. He took aim. Then he heaved the harpoon. *Pffft!* It sailed high and hit the roof, right where it needed to.

Then Ned pulled a cord that lit the dynamite.

"He's got just enough time," the professor whispered. "He can be back before it explodes."

Ned turned around, moving quickly, and hurried back toward the submarine.

But suddenly, the harpoon fell down! If the dynamite on the end of the harpoon was not placed exactly on the roof of the creature's mouth, the plan wouldn't work! He had to go back and shoot again! Ned stopped and crawled back toward the harpoon.

Beth groaned. "He'll never make it now."

20,000 LEAGUES UNDER THE SEA

Any second and the dynamite would explode.

Ned picked up the harpoon and flung it again, harder this time.

Thwack! The point sunk into the roof. This time, it stuck hard. The creature thrashed about.

Ned wheeled around. He crawled as quickly as he could back to the submarine.

Then there was an earsplitting explosion as the dynamite went off. The monster twisted and bucked. Its mouth ripped open.

With a loud *whoosh*, the submarine floated free at last.

Beth pressed her nose against the glass. "Ned!" She cried. Ned was still inside the creature's mouth! She saw him roll over and over. And then he disappeared.

"Ned!" she shouted.

She raced to the hatch. The professor and Nemo trailed behind. Then Nemo flung open the door.

"Ned!" Beth screamed again.

CHAPTER 15

There was no answer. He was gone.

The submarine floated free and everything was quiet again. They looked out the hatch, but it seemed as if Ned was gone. The professor hugged Beth tightly as they looked out of the hatch. Nemo hesitated. Then he put an arm around them both, trying to make them feel better.

Suddenly one hand gripped the ladder.

The professor glanced up. "Ned?" he called.

Ned climbed inside, grinning.

"Thank goodness!" Beth exclaimed.

The professor clapped him on the back. "Bravo!"

"I told you!" Ned threw back his shoulders.

"I'm the best harpoonist to sail the seas."

Nemo saluted him. "Thank you for saving us," he said.

"Now, Captain," the professor said to Nemo, "are you a man of your word?"

Nemo kept quiet, thinking.

"*Mobilis in mobile?*" asked Beth.

"Yes!" Nemo said, and smiled. "You shall be free in a free world."

A few minutes later, the *Nautilus* climbed to the surface. Nemo's crew pushed out a rowboat, and the professor, Beth, and Ned scrambled inside. They would soon be free.

It had been quite an adventure. They had set out on a journey, discovered a new kind of life under the sea, come face-to-face with a sea creature, and survived it all.

They heard a faint ship's whistle in the distance. They knew that the USS *Abraham Lincoln* would be there soon to pick them up.

The professor couldn't wait to get back and record his

findings. Beth was ready to add her own thoughts on the creature, too. Ned was just glad to get back to his ship. But they all had made a promise to Nemo to keep the submarine a secret, and they would all keep their word.